For Mom & Dad—Maria Antonietta Martinez & José León Virján—*con cariño*

Library of Congress Control Number: 2015936055
ISBN 978-0-06-241528-8

The artist used charcoal sketches painted digitally to create the illustrations for this book.
Typography by Dana Fritts
15 16 17 18 19   SCP   10 9 8 7 6 5 4 3 2 1
❖ First Edition

WHAT THIS STORY NEEDS IS

A HUSH AND A SHUSH

By Emma J. Virján

HARPER

An Imprint of HarperCollinsPublishers

What this bedtime needs is
a pig in a wig,

brushing
her teeth,

combing
her hair,

and going to bed
with her pink
teddy bear.

This bedtime also
needs a quack,
a honk,

a neigh,
and a moo,

a cluck,

a hiss,

a peep,

and a pig in a wig
who is trying to sleep.

Be quiet. Keep mum.
Pipe down and **HUSH!**
What this bedtime needs
is a **SHUSH!**

Back to your beds without . . .
a quack, a honk,
a bark, a coo,

a ribbit, a meow,
a neigh, or a moo.

No more
cluck, hiss,
baa, or peep.

It's late at night
and we all need our sleep.

What this bedtime
needs now is . . .

a quieter place to sleep.

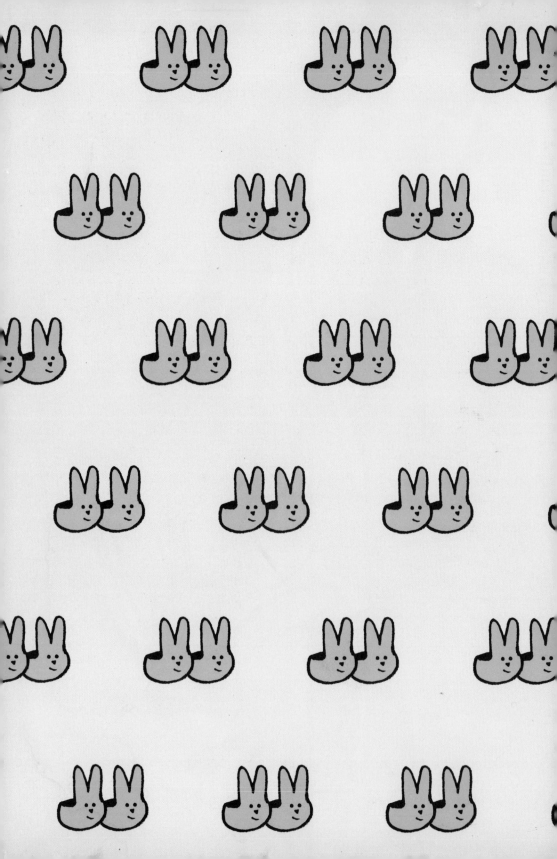